47625 Baker & Taylor 7/24/01

I like trains that hoot and roar
as they rumble by my door.

First come engines, big and strong,

pulling lots of cars along.

Some cars keep things from the rain.

Some cars carry trucks or grain,

or cows

or hogs

or gas

or logs.

Some carry steel; some carry scrap,

or secret stuff that's under wrap.

But the best car's at the end,
and as the train goes round the bend,

I wave.

I'm glad

to see the car that carries Dad.

Trains, trains, trains!

I LOVE trains!

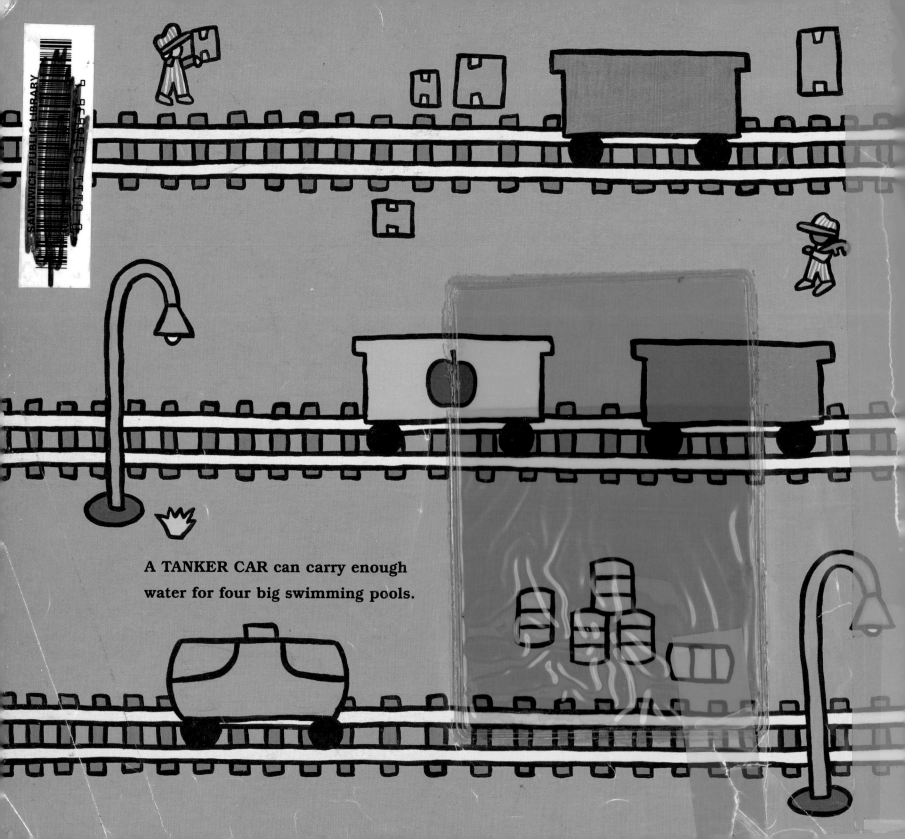

A TANKER CAR can carry enough water for four big swimming pools.